Special Delivery

By Mara Conlon

SCHOLASTIC INC.

New York   Toronto   London   Auckland   Sydney
Mexico City   New Delhi   Hong Kong   Buenos Aires

ISBN-13: 978-0-545-01325-3
ISBN-10: 0-545-01325-9

Based on the TV series *Wow! Wow! Wubbzy!* as seen
on Nick Jr.®, created by Bob Boyle.

Published by Scholastic Inc. SCHOLASTIC and
associated logos are trademarks and/or registered
trademarks of Scholastic Inc.

12 11 10 9 8 7 6 5 4 3 2   8 9 10 11/0

Designed by Kim Brown

Printed in the U.S.A.
First printing, May 2008

"Choo-choo!" said Wubbzy.
"Wow! I love trains!"

Choo-
choo!

Ding-dong. The doorbell rang.
"I have a special delivery,"
said the mailman.

Ding-
dong!

"Is it for me?" said Wubbzy.
"No, it is for Walden," said the
mailman. "Can you keep it for him?"
"Yes!" said Wubbzy.

TO:
WALDEN

Wubbzy wanted to know
what was inside.
Choo-choo!
His train hit the box.
The box opened.

Choo-choo!

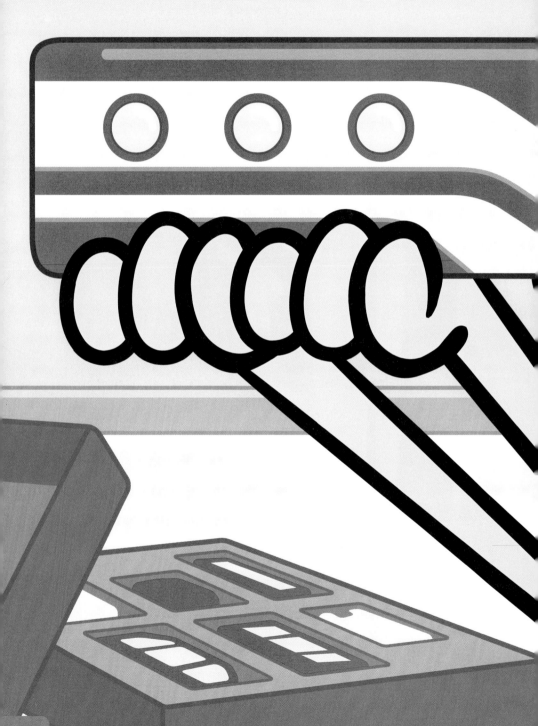

"Wow!" said Wubbzy.
"A train!"
Wubbzy took it out.
"I will see if it works,"
he said.

The train went around the room!
Ding-dong.
"Oh, no!" said Wubbzy.
"What if Walden is here?"

Widget opened the door.
Toot-toot!
The train went by.

Toot-toot!

"Is this your train?" said Widget.
"No," said Wubbzy. "It is Walden's."

14

"You should not play with it without asking,"
Widget said.
They put the tracks back in the box.
Wubbzy shut the box.

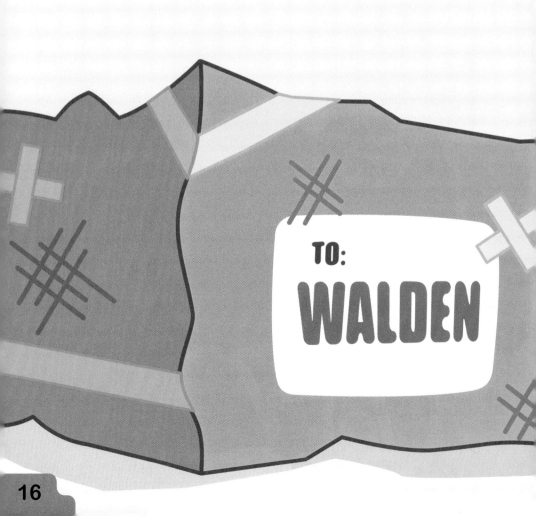

TO:
WALDEN

Toot-toot!
**They forgot the train!
It went out the door.**

Toot-toot!

"Oh, no!" they said.
The train went this way.
The train went that way.

Wubbzy saw Walden.
Wubbzy ran to the front of the house.
"Hi," said Walden.
"I am here for my box."

"I am sorry," Wubbzy said.
"I opened your box. Now the train
is going everywhere!"

Walden took something
out of the box.
"You need this," he said.
Walden stopped
the train.

"I am sorry I played with your train," said Wubbzy.
"The train is a gift for you!" said Walden.
"Thanks!" said Wubbzy.

"I can fix it," said Widget.

"I love both my trains!" said Wubbzy.